I Think That Next Time.....
I Will Hold Mummy's Hand

by

Jenny Warden

Illustrated by Irene Joslin

AuthorHouse™ UK Ltd.
500 Avebury Boulevard
Central Milton Keynes, MK9 2BE
www.authorhouse.co.uk
Phone: 08001974150

First published by AuthorHouse 9/16/2008

ISBN: 978-1-4343-9719-5 (sc)

Printed in the United States of America
Bloomington, Indiana

This book is printed on acid-free paper.

authorHOUSE®

I think that next time I will hold mummy's hand, which is so safe and secure.

I think that next time I will know better.

Like the time we went to the big superstore.
Instead of holding mummy's hand like she
asked, I ran off to have my own adventure.

So many things all bright and colourful,
lots of things to see. It was all exciting
for a few minutes. I think I am quite big
and grown-up now that I am four.

But suddenly everyone looks so big and scary…. Where is my mummy?

Not in this big aisle, and not
around that corner either.

Too many faces, too many things!

Just as I am getting really scared, there she is!

Mummy has a worried
look on her face, and
her hand held out
to hold on to mine.

I think that next time I will just hold her hand, so safe and secure.

But silly me, I made a fuss, stepped
out and nearly met with the bus!

If it wasn't for mummy and her lovely strong hand, pulling me back to safer ground, I think I would have been a pancake as flat as can be! I should have known better.

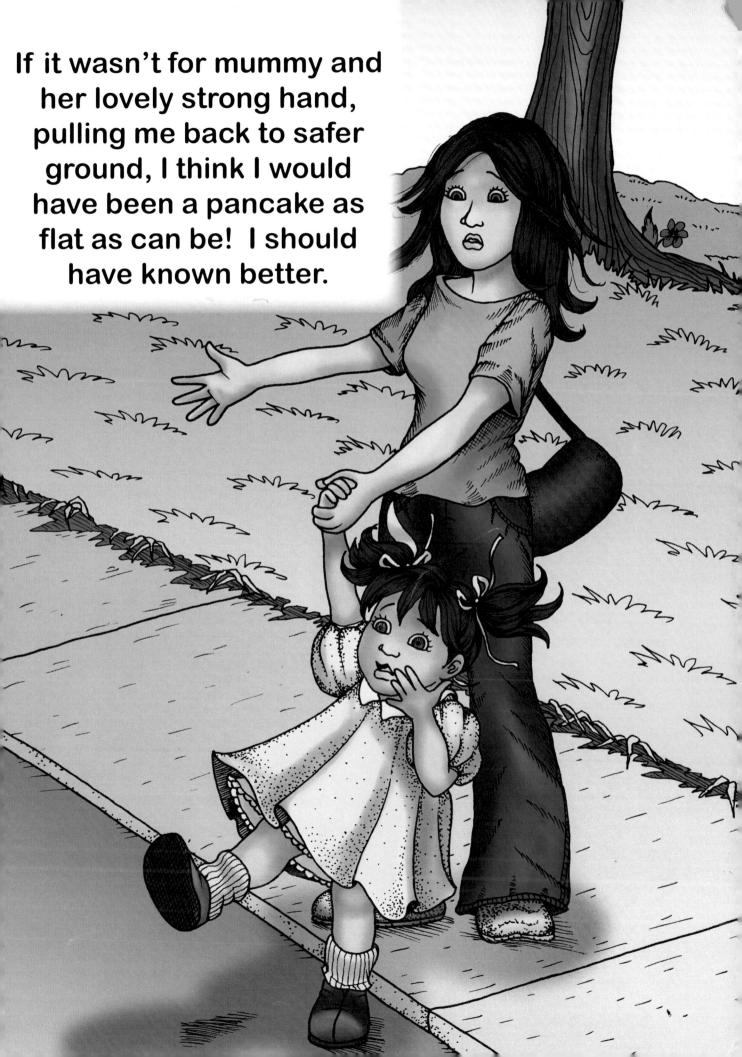

I think that the next time I am asked, I will hold mummy's hand, which is so safe and secure.

I like to hold my mummy's hand. It is so soft
and warm. It feels good when I feel a bit
unsure and need to feel a bit more secure.
It's always there so safe and strong.

So you know, I think I will always hold mummy's hand!

CPSIA information can be obtained
at www.ICGtesting.com
Printed in the USA
388426LV00022B/214